Snow-White
and the 7 Dwarfs

Illustrations by J. L. MACIAS S.

Retold by JANE CARRUTH

Once upon a time there was a young Princess called Snow-White whose mother had died soon after she was born.

Snow-White's father, the King, married again. His new Queen was a strange woman, tall and beautiful, but with the powers of a witch. In a secret room at the top of the palace were hidden her Book of Magic Spells, her raven and her black pot of magic potions.

On the wall hung a magic mirror. Every day the Queen looked into her magic mirror and asked it the same question: "Mirror, mirror on the wall, who is the fairest of us all?" And the mirror would reply: "You, O Queen, are the fairest of all."

Then one day, the magic mirror
told the proud Queen that
Snow-White was now the fairest
in the land. "Then she must die!" cried the Queen in a rage. And she sent for
one of her huntsmen and told him to take the girl into the forest and kill her.
But the huntsman could not do such a cruel thing.

He told Snow-White to hide away in the forest. Soon after he left her, Snow-White came upon a little cottage among the trees. When she opened the door and looked inside, she saw seven little chairs around the untidy breakfast table.

In the room upstairs, Snow-White found seven little beds and, with a huge yawn, she lay down and was soon fast asleep. She was still asleep when the seven little dwarfs came home from the gold and diamond mines where they worked. How surprised they were to find Snow-White in their cottage.

"Who can she be?" they asked each other in wonderment.

The dwarfs waited patiently until Snow-White opened her eyes. When they heard her sad story, the eldest said, "You may stay here if you promise to cook for us and keep the cottage tidy."

"I should love to," said Snow-White. And from that day she became the dwarfs' housekeeper and took care of them.

Now the wicked Queen soon learned from her magic mirror that
Snow-White still lived and, disguising herself as an old country
woman, she hurried to the cottage. "I have brought you a lovely rosy-red
apple, pretty one," she croaked when she saw Snow-White.
Alas, the apple contained a deadly poison.

No sooner did Snow-White take a bite of the poisoned apple than she fell to the ground. The seven dwarfs wept bitter tears when they came home from the mines and found her.

"This is the work of the evil Queen," said one, shaking his head. "She is too beautiful to lie buried in the cold earth," said another. "Let us make her a glass coffin so that all who pass this way may see how beautiful she is!"

And that is what the seven sad little dwarfs did! Day and night, two sat by the glass coffin on guard until, one day, a handsome Prince came riding through the forest.

The Prince fell so deeply in love with Snow-White that he begged the dwarfs to allow his servants to take her back to his palace. And, at last, they agreed. But when the glass coffin was moved the piece of poisoned apple, lodged in her throat, fell from her mouth. She was alive! Overcome with joy, the Prince told Snow-White that he loved her with all his heart.

Soon after, the noble Prince carried Snow-White away on his white charger. The seven little dwarfs were sad to see her go, but when they attended her wedding the next week, they danced for joy!

Published in United States and simultaneously in Canada by Joshua Morris, Inc.
431 Post Road East, Westport, CT 06880
Printed in Belgium